THE TANGLEWEED

TROLL

Cliff Wright

LONDON • VICTOR GOLLANCZ • 1993

Beyond the garden gate
my friends called me to play,

but Daddy said I couldn't go
because of all the wizards

and giants
and pirates
out there,
and the Tangleweed Troll
who'd take me home for supper
if I stepped in the woods.

But I said,
"Daddy, maybe you're a troll,"
and he just smiled and said,
"Jenny, don't let me see you
go outside the garden gate,"

and so he never looked
when I did.

Perhaps I heard a wily wizard call,
"I wonder where can Jenny be?"

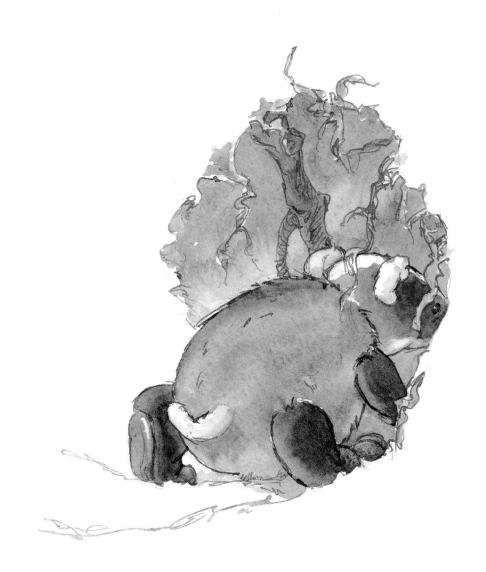

"Are you up there . . .

scampering with the squirrels?"

"No! I'm down here,

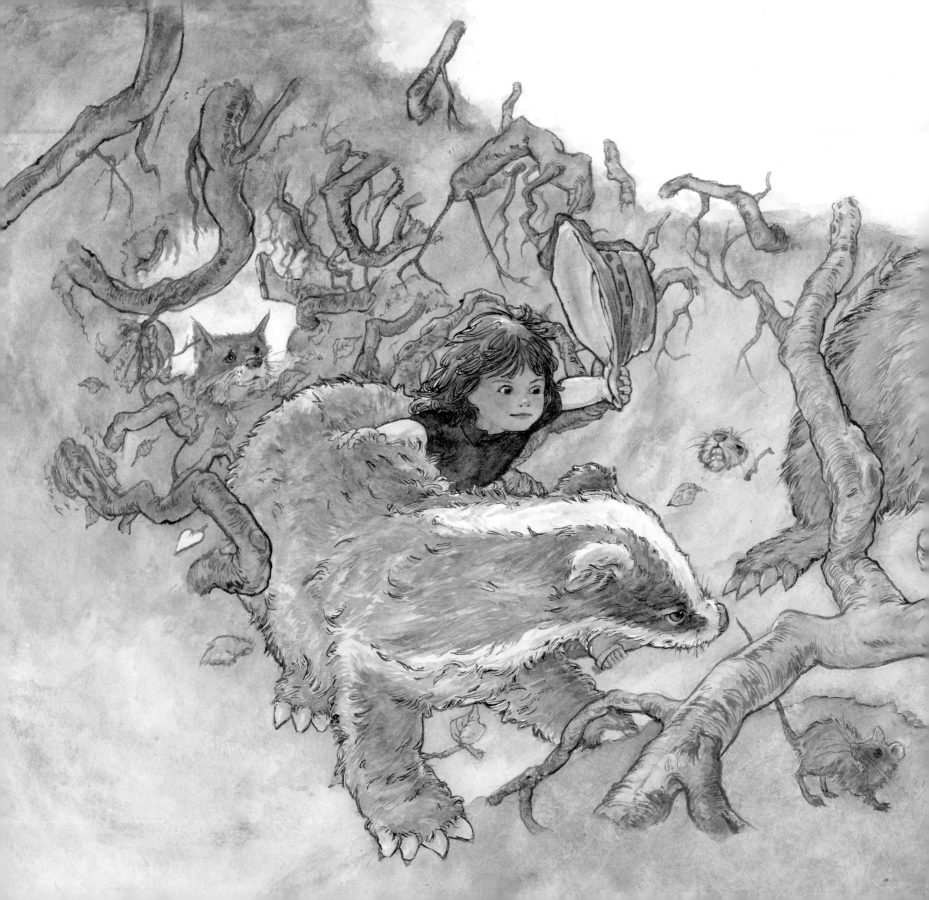

tracking the Tangleweed Troll."

Perhaps I heard a jumbled giant roar,
"Wherever can that Jenny be?"

"Are you over there . . .

romping with the rabbits?"

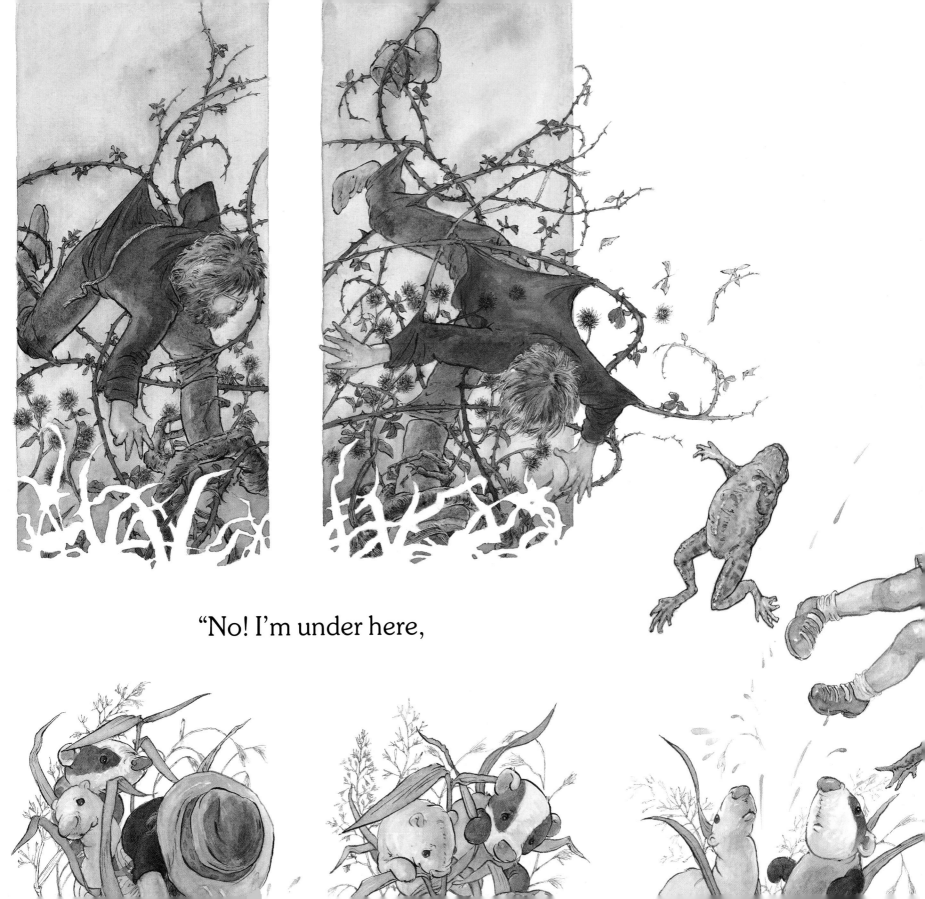

"No! I'm under here,

teasing the
Tangleweed
Troll."

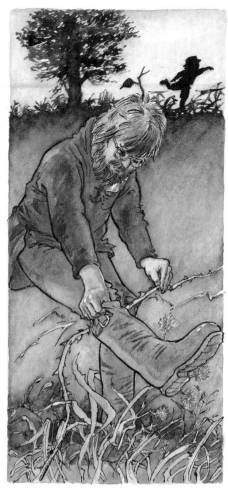

Perhaps I heard a pesky pirate shout,
"Now where on earth can Jenny be?"

"Are you in there . . .

frolicking with the fishes?"

"No! I'm out here,

tricking the Tangleweed Troll."

But suddenly
my happy game was through,
as all my secret friends
deserted me.

Perhaps they'd heard . . .

the stamping, trampling tread   of *my* Tangleweed Troll

who'd come to take me home

for supper.

First published in Great Britain 1993
by Victor Gollancz, an imprint of Cassell
Villiers House, 41/47 Strand, London WC2N 5JE

Copyright © 1993 Cliff Wright

The right of Cliff Wright to be identified as author of this work
has been asserted by him in accordance with the Copyright, Designs
and Patents Act 1988

A catalogue record for this book is available from the British Library

ISBN 0 575 05491 3

*All rights reserved. No reproduction, copy or transmission of this
publication may be made without prior written permission and this
publication or any part of it, shall not, by way of trade or otherwise,
be made up for sale, or re-sold or otherwise circulated in any other form
than that in which it is published.*

Printed and bound in Hong Kong by Imago Publishing Ltd